Read On

A Big Surprise

Celia Warren

QED Publishing

First published in the UK in 2005 by
QED Publishing
A Quarto Group company
226 City Road
London EC1V 2TT
www.qed-publishing.co.uk

A Catalogue record for this book is available from the British Library.

ISBN 1 84538 172 6

Written by Celia Warren
Designed by Zeta Jones
Editor Hannah Ray
Photographer Michael Wicks

With thanks to Alice, Amy, Tarina,
Billy, Harrison and Danny.

Series Consultant Anne Faundez
Publisher Steve Evans
Creative Director
   Louise Morley
Editorial Manager
   Jean Coppendale

Printed and bound
in China

Cast List

Kim

Jack

Molly

Sanjay

Leela

Bear

Props
- Three teddy bears (one big teddy, one small teddy and one teddy wearing a green bow tie)
- A toy rabbit
- A picnic blanket
- A plate of apples
- A plate of fairy cakes
- A plate of samosas
- A bottle of squash
- Picnic plates and cups

Setting
The play takes place in a clearing in a wood.

(Enter Kim and Jack. Kim carrying big teddy bear and blanket, Jack carrying apples and plates.)

Jack: Here we are. The meeting place for the teddy bears' picnic!

Kim: *(Looking around)* I wonder where everybody is.

Jack: *(Excitedly)* I expect they'll be here soon.

Kim: *(Spreading blanket and adding apples)* Where's your teddy?

Jack: *(Pulling small bear from pocket)* Here he is.

Kim: Ooh, he's tiny, isn't he? What's his name?

Jack: He's called Teddy.

Kim: So is mine. *(Making bear wave)* Hello, Tiny Teddy.

Jack: *(Making bear wave back)* Hello, Big Teddy.

5

(Enter Molly carrying bear and bottle of squash and cups.)

Molly: *(Speaking in bear's ear)* It's OK, Teddy, we're not lost. The picnic's here. *(Waving bottle)* Hello, are we late?

Jack: No, we haven't started yet.

Kim: *(Pointing at Molly's bear)* Is he called Teddy?

Molly: Yes. What are your bears called?

Jack and Kim: *(Together)* Teddy!

Molly: It IS a popular name, but we can tell them apart. My teddy has a green bow tie.

Jack: *(Showing Molly)* My teddy fits in my pocket.

Kim: (*Showing Molly*) And my teddy fits on my lap.

Molly: Well, my teddy fits … (*putting bear and bottle on picnic blanket*) … here!

(*All arrange teddies on blanket and hand round apples.*)

(Enter Sanjay carrying cakes and toy rabbit.)

Sanjay: This looks like the teddy bears' picnic. *(To others)* Hi, everyone.

Jack: *(Showing his teddy)* Hello. Have you got a teddy bear?

Kim: *(Showing her teddy)* We have.

Molly: *(Holding up her teddy)* And mine's got a green bow tie.

Sanjay: *(Holding up rabbit)* He's not as smart as mine.

Molly: *(Pointing)* But that's not a teddy bear. That's a rabbit.

Sanjay: *(Frowning)* He IS a teddy bear. It's just he's got long ears.

Kim: Is he called Teddy?

Sanjay: No, he's called Bunny, (*proudly*) Bunny Bear!

Jack: (*Smiling*) Bunny Bear the funny bear!

(*All laugh kindly. Sanjay puts cakes on blanket.*)

Kim: I know – why don't we all play a game?

Sanjay: Or we could have a race.

Jack: Yes. Let's have a bear race.

Molly: A BARE race? (*Folding arms*) I'm not getting undressed.

Jack: Not that sort of 'bare' – a TEDDY bear race.

Kim: What's a teddy bear race?

Jack: (*Bending one knee and gripping bear, ready to run*) It's like a normal running race except that it starts, 'Ready, TEDDY, Go!'
(*Begins to run in wide circles.*)

Molly and Kim: Ready, Teddy, Go!

(*They run around the stage.*)

Sanjay: (*Pausing to look at his rabbit*) Runny, Bunny, GO!

(*Sanjay runs after the others.*)

Bear: (*Loudly, off-stage*) GRRRR!

(*All bump to a sudden standstill.*)

Sanjay: (*Startled*) What was that?

Kim: I d-d-d-don't know!

Bear: (*Still off-stage*) GRRRR!

Molly: Whatever is it?

Jack: (*Nervously*) It's ... it's a ... it's ... er ... GETTING CLOSER!

Bear: (*Very loudly, still off-stage*) GRRRR!

(*All scream and hang on to their bears, except Sanjay, who drops Bunny Bear.*)

13

(*Enter Leela carrying a plate of samosas.*)

Leela: (*Laying plate on picnic blanket*) Is this the teddy bears' picnic?

Jack: (*As group relaxes*) Yes. We were just panicking (*coughs*), I mean picnicking, when we heard …

Leela: (*Putting hands to her face*) Heard what?

Kim: (*Quickly, before Jack can reply*) … heard YOU coming!

Leela: Oh, that's all right then. I thought I heard a growling sound.

(*All laugh nervously but begin sharing picnic.*)

15

Jack: (*Showing Leela*) This is Teddy. He's the smallest bear at the picnic.

Kim: (*Showing Leela*) And this is my bear. He's called Teddy, too. He's the biggest bear here.

Molly: (*Making her bear jump up and down*) And this is Teddy, too. He's got a green bow tie.

Sanjay: And this is Bunny Bear. He's got the longest ears.

Kim: (*To Leela*) Where's your teddy bear?

Molly: Did you forget him?

Leela: (*Sadly*) I'm afraid I haven't got a bear.

Sanjay: (*Pointing a shaky finger off-stage*) Oh yes, you have!

Bear: (*Running on stage, growling loudly*)
GRRRRRR!

(*All scream and exit, dropping bears.*)

Bear: (*Alone, looking bewildered, circling the picnic blanket and licking his lips.*)
(*Very softly*) Grrr?

Bear collects teddies and arranges them around blanket, sitting with them.

Bear: (*Feeding himself and the teddy next to him.*)
(*Happily*)
Grrr ... UB!

What do you think?

How many children came to the teddy bears' picnic?

Can you remember all the picnic foods?

Who did not have
a teddy bear?

Where did Jack
keep his teddy?

Can you find
two words
which sound
the same
but mean
different things?

What was funny
about Sanjay's
'teddy bear'?

Which word means 'the most big'?

Why do you think Jack said 'panicking' when he meant to say 'picnicking'?

Parents' and teachers' notes

- Explain to your child that a play is acted in front of an audience but that it can also be fun simply to read the play aloud.
- Look at the cast list on page 3. Explain that the cast list is a list of all the characters that appear in the play.
- Look at the props list on the same page. Tell your child that props are objects that actors use in a play.
- Find examples of stage directions throughout the script (*in italics*). Explain to your child that these directions tell the actors what to do.
- Draw attention to the use of punctuation, capital letters, brackets and adverbs. How are these used in the playscript?
- Encourage your child to choose one of the characters from the play. Read through the play, helping your child to read his or her lines while you read the other parts.
- Choose a section of the play and practise reading it aloud. Experiment with expression and pace.
- Examine how the text reflects each character's personality. Does the group have a natural leader?

- Choose a costume for each character. Look through the script and check for any special features that will need to be included, e.g. Jack's pocket. How could a bear costume be created? Discuss using face paint as an alternative to a mask.
- Plan a backdrop to the 'stage'. How could you make it look like a woodland?
- Consider introducing non-speaking parts so that more children can join in. What might they bring to the picnic?
- Search out poems and songs about teddy bears to complement the play. Can you find a piece of music to play at the end?
- Use the text to introduce the concept of relative sizes and related vocabulary, e.g. 'tiny', 'biggest', etc.
- Draw attention to the use of wordplay – homophones (words which sound the same but have different meanings, e.g. 'bear' and 'bare'), rhymes and puns.
- Does your child have a favourite bear/toy? What is its name? Conduct a survey to find the most popular teddy bear name in your child's class or school.